Mewingham
MANOR

*Dedicated to my family for their support,
encouragement, and, in some cases, inspiration.*

Special thanks to Scott Usher, Wendy Wentworth, Deborah Cannarella, Sheryl Kober,
and the rest of the creative team at The Greenwich Workshop.

A GREENWICH WORKSHOP PRESS BOOK
Copyright ©2002 The Greenwich Workshop, Inc.
Artwork ©2002 Laura Von Stetina

Published by the Greenwich Workshop, Inc. One Greenwich Place, P.O. Box 875, Shelton, CT 06484. (800) 243-4246
www.greenwichworkshop.com

Library of Congress Cataloging-in-Publication Data

Von Stetina, Laura
   Mewingham Manor : observations on a curious new species / by Edwina Von Stetina.
      p. cm.
   ISBN 0-86713-082-2
   1. Inheritance and succession—Fiction. 2. Animal experimentation—Fiction.
   3. Country homes—Fiction. 4. Cats—Fiction. I. Title.

PS3622.O67 M49 2002
813'.6—dc21   2002068641

Laura Von Stetina's three-dimensional collectible figurines are available through The Greenwich Workshop, Inc.,
and its 1,200 dealers in North America. Visit our website at www.greenwichworkshop.com to learn the location
of the dealer nearest to you or contact the publisher at the address above.

Edited by Deborah Cannarella and Wendy Wentworth
Photography by Bob Hixon
Artwork on the endleaf and page seven, courtesy of Cortney Skinner
Book design by Maria Miller Design
Manufactured in Japan by Toppan
First Printing 2002
1 2 3 4 5   04 03 02 01

Mewingham
MANOR

Observations on a Curious New Species

by Edwina Von Stetina

The Greenwich Workshop Press

Edwina Fitzhugh Von Stetina

London, January 1875

March 10, 1875

I begin this journal as I begin this new chapter of my life. After three days of travel by carriage from London, I have arrived at what is to be my new home, the rambling country estate bequeathed to me by my seafaring uncle, Captain Bartholomew Katt.

Uncle Katt was the most adventurous and mysterious member of the family, a "black sheep," Mother always said, who left home at age fourteen for a life at sea. Grandfather told me that, even as a child, Uncle loved to study flora and fauna. Although Uncle cherished his life aboard ship, he most loved his travels to distant lands, where he would seek out exotic life forms.

How wonderful that this uncle I was forbidden to know would leave me this unimaginable gift—his secluded Mewingham Manor!—although I do wonder at the significance of the unusual name.

Sir Percy Landsworth, Uncle's solicitor, said it has been more than three years since Uncle has been home. He is presumed lost at sea with his ship, the Flying Tiger. Only his trunk was found, and it was returned to London last winter on a schooner from West Africa. I am eager to look inside and learn all I can about my dear uncle.

It's strange to be suddenly living in quiet isolation. I will miss my apprenticeship with Miss Jekyll, as we were making such progress on the Clematis series. I feel a pang of guilt at leaving Mother, too, but now at least I spare her the embarrassment of explaining why her only child is yet unmarried, at the late age of twenty-seven. My studies of plants, insects, and other creatures of the natural world filled my life and left me with little time or interest in London society.

From my window I can see the ancient apple orchards, the pastures, woodlands, and formal gardens. They are filled with the dazzling colors of butterflies and blossoms. I will surely be busy here for many years. Perhaps I will discover a new Wood White or Silver-studded Blue and finally read my name in the Linnean Society's esteemed journal!

I am grateful that the small staff here has agreed to remain. The housekeeper, groundskeeper, and cook have been at the manor for decades. Cook said that Uncle Bartholomew—she calls him "Captain"—brought back many unusual plants and specimens. She was oddly silent when I pressed her for details, perhaps feeling her own ignorance under my scrutiny, and I was immediately sorry to have inquired. So, I will explore on my own. I can hardly wait to begin!

I spied two carved stone gateposts as the coachman turned the horses down the drive.

March 11, 1875

I slept very soundly through the night, undisturbed by a single dream, even though my favorite coverlet is still to arrive. This morning, however, I awoke with a start, and it took me a moment to know where I was.

I knew immediately I was not at home. The furnishings are quite unlike those I am accustomed to, and quite unlike any I have seen. The bedroom pieces are made from the English walnut tree (Juglans regia). I saw these trees in the woods beyond the gates as the coach arrived—a lovely species native to South Britain, and, curiously, also to the Himalayas. What most struck me about these pieces is that, although made in the Queen Anne style, known for its carved ball-and-claw foot, they had an unusual variation. Instead of a bird's claw, it was a cat's paw that clutched the ball! Whoever designed these must have loved cats. It suddenly occurs to me that this eccentric designer might have been my very own uncle. These are not the first feline embellishments I have seen. Even as I arrived at the front door yesterday, I stopped for a moment before raising the knocker to admire its unusual design.

The bedroom is charming in every way, but I see a light coating of dust in the strong sunlight. The house-keeper must have grown lax with so few inhabitants these

The eyes are screws that fasten the plate to the door.

past years—but I notice here and there a spot or two that seems newly polished, in patches, as if, well, almost as if tiny paws had pranced across the surface. Oh, my imagination runs away with me—yet this intriguing place would surely launch even the most sober of visitors on winged flights of fancy.

I wonder what the house cat, Mr. Grimes, makes of the winged sculptures that surround my bedroom window?

April 2, 1875

Columbine (Aquilegia)

A most astonishing day! By early afternoon, the last of the rain clouds had fled, and brilliant sunlight sparkled on the meadows. I could not contain my curiosity and ventured out of the house with my sketchbook.

I wanted to explore the early spring blossoms in the gardens today, but an unusual hedgerow border had caught my eye from the window, some sort of dwarf evergreen I had never seen. Before reaching the hedge, I stopped to examine an intriguing pattern of insect damage on the branches of an old rose bush. As I bent to look more closely, I heard a sudden, violent thrashing in the branches above. An amazing creature landed softly on the branch before my eyes and, teetering for an instant, clung tightly for balance. It was tiny, with fluffy, black and white fur, and, although by all other evidence a mammal, it wore a pair of dazzling jewel-toned wings!

The startled creature held perfectly still for a moment, gazing back at me with wide, bright, black eyes. Then, it thrashed about in much agitation, let go of its hold, and fluttered unsteadily downward. The wings began to beat rhythmically,

Found wing,
perhaps the Delias
butterfly, indigenous to Asia

The wings seemed to have the same pattern as the
Euxanthe butterfly, which is native to Africa, but
the shades were much brighter and much
more beautiful!

Euxanthe crossleyi

I never felt alone in the gardens—and
sometimes even had the feeling that
I was being watched.

Creature's wing shape
resembled the White Peacock
butterfly (Anartia jatrophae).

I wonder if this wing belongs to the Small Tortoiseshell Butterfly (Aglais urticae), whose population is now in decline.

and the amazing creature was soon hovering about my knees. Suddenly, with a powerful, quick flick of its wings, it glided off, in fine form, seeming no worse for the encounter.

I was less fortunate. I released the breath that had caught in my throat, steadied myself against a nearby stump, and sat, marveling for a long while at what I thought I had seen. I then had the presence of mind to make some quick sketches and color studies, while the images were still vivid in my memory (although I doubt I could forget them in a lifetime).

I must remember to wear my sturdy bonnet on future walks in the event strange little animals again rain from the trees.

Earlier today, I noticed swarms of what I thought to be large butterflies dancing in the distance. I had not yet been close enough to determine what species they were, and expected to discover them busily feeding on the abundant clover blossoms. Is it possible these flying creatures might also have fur and ears and tails? This afternoon has been quite unsettling. Perhaps I will ask Cook to forego afternoon tea in favor of a bracing hot toddy.

Foreleg

Forewing

Thorax

Fly Amanita
(Amanita muscaria)

After my restorative "tea," I ventured out to discover the creature again, which was now less agitated and perched comfortably on top of a mushroom in a soggy patch at the orchard's edge. It let me come quite close to inspect it and did not stir.

It was then that I finally understood! This tiny miracle was not a relative of the butterfly at all, but a unique species of its own, and here was its natural habitat. The delicate wings held all the colors of the mushroom upon which it sat! I suspect the little mushroom dweller feeds on the fungi as well—and, in inclement weather, can nestle safely beneath its broad cap. I must make an accurate painting!

April 3, 1875

I can still scarcely believe what I have seen!
A creature unlike anything I have known or read of in books. Am I truly the
first to find it? Surely, one of the staff here—the groundskeeper, perhaps—has
encountered this tiny animal while tending the gardens. Clearly, the winged sculptures
about the manor are not mere creatures of whimsy. My uncle had seen them, too!

I must search the library. It is just as Uncle left it, and perhaps there I will find
answers to these bewildering questions. His desk is open, and a pen lies by the inkwell.
His eyeglasses are still folded on the blotter, as if he had just left off reading for a walk
in the woods and will return at any moment. In one of the side drawers, I found a small
key, itself a curiosity. I searched the room for a drawer or box the key might open. In
the corner stood the large trunk that had survived Uncle's shipwreck. The key worked!

The trunk was filled with clothing and many books and papers, somehow
untouched by the sea. I dug deep into the contents and found a small box. It held a few
coins, a button, and a miniature portrait of a man, painted in watercolors, to fit
a lady's locket—but whose? On the back was faintly inscribed, "Bartholomew,
1845." I also found a small rolled map, tied with ribbon, and a stack of old
books, hand written and leather bound, whose edges appeared to be chewed.
These were the ship's logs and journals, records of my uncle's journeys. As
I began to read, the mysteries of the manor began to unfold.

Uncle Katt, as a young sea captain, in his forty-third year

The Flying Tiger, 1845

Fine day. Strong winds. Today, the Flying Tiger sets sail from the

East India docks, London, with 42 crew, for destinations known and

unknown. My studies are unfinished, and there is still much left to learn.

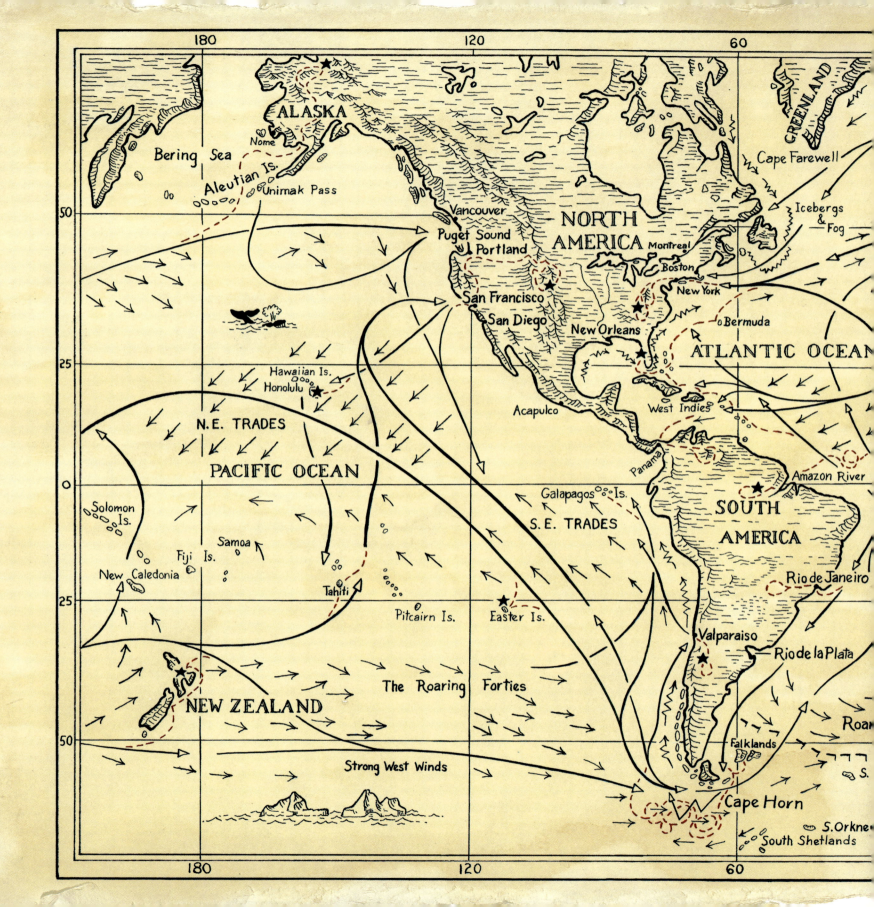

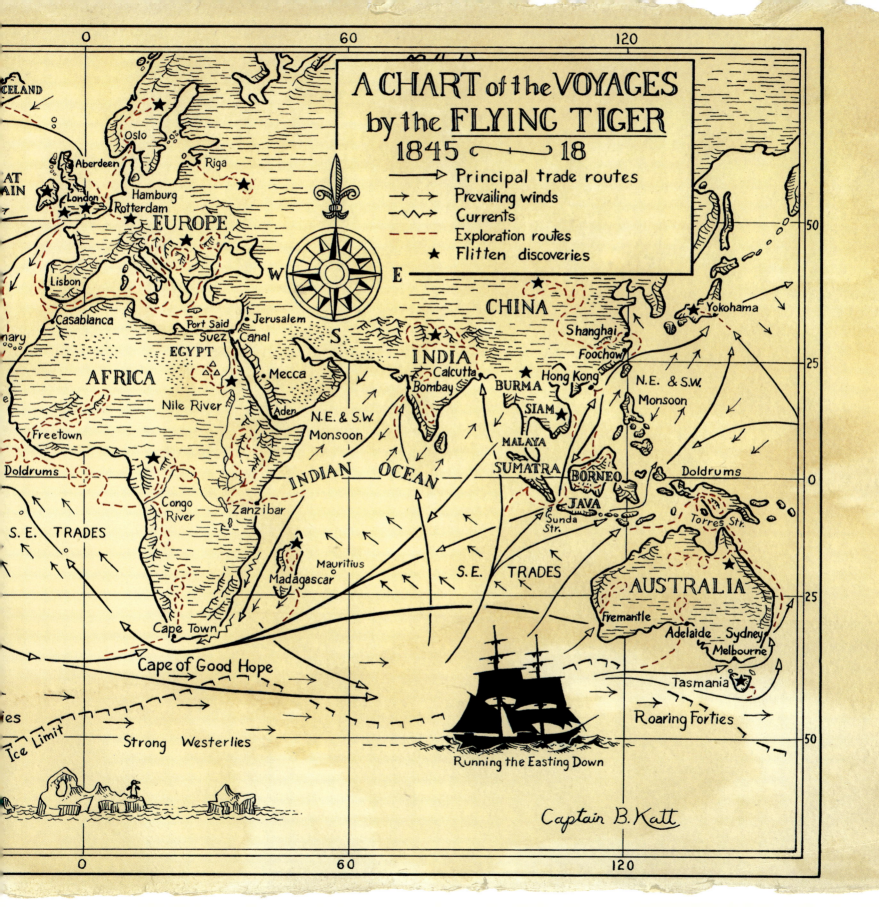

A CHART of the VOYAGES by the FLYING TIGER 1845 ⌐ 18

⟶	Principal trade routes
→	Prevailing winds
∿	Currents
---	Exploration routes
★	Flitten discoveries

ICELAND

Oslo

Aberdeen

Riga

AT AIN

London   Hamburg   Rotterdam

Lisbon

EUROPE

W · E

S

CHINA

Casablanca

Port Said   · Jerusalem
Suez   Canal

EGYPT

· Mecca

Shanghai

INDIA

Foochow

Yokohama

AFRICA

Nile River

Aden

Calcutta

Bombay

Hong Kong

BURMA

SIAM

N.E. & S.W.
Monsoon

nary

Freetown

N.E. & S.W.
Monsoon

MALAYA

SUMATRA

BORNEO

Doldrums

Doldrums

INDIAN   OCEAN

JAVA

Congo
River

Zanzibar

Sunda
Str.

Torres Str.

S.E. TRADES

Mauritius

Madagascar

AUSTRALIA

S.E.   TRADES

Cape Town

Fremantle

Adelaide   Sydney
Melbourne

Cape of Good Hope

Tasmania

Roaring Forties

ies

Ice Limit   Strong Westerlies

Running the Easting Down

Captain B. Katt

April 4, 1875

I took breakfast early this morning in the dining room.
My head was still reeling from my discovery the evening before, and although
grateful for some quiet time to reflect, I was distracted by the persistent pokings of
an odd-looking fly. I thought I had succeeded in brushing it away, but it alighted
on the very hand in which I held my spoon. It was then that I saw it was not a fly
at all, but a miniscule mouse with wings! It had a small furry body, shell-like pink

ears, a long graceful pink tail, four dainty little feet, and bright sparkling
eyes that seemed to be laughing at me—cheeky little thing! After a
moment, he twitched his tiny pink nose and flew off with a
flutter of iridescent wings.

I was still gaping at the spot where the creature had been
when Cook suddenly entered the room, asking if I would have

more tea. She stopped speaking when she saw my face, and seemed at first alarmed, and then quite amused. "I see ye have found us out, Miss," she said. To encourage her to continue, I invited her to sit.

Cook was a young girl, just arrived from Scotland, when Uncle hired her. She soon noticed the strange creatures flying "to and fro" about the manor, she said, but she thought they were just the sort of thing one found in England, never before having been out of the Highlands herself.

"So you have seen the tiny winged cat, too?" I asked her.

"Aye," she said, "and there be others all about. I don't pay them much mind anymore. The wee mice are a handful of trouble, though, Miss. Always bothering the kittens and Mr. Grimes, the old house cat, you know, who gets in such a state he makes a terrible stir in me pantry, toppling parcels, his fur flying everywhere. Those rogues have run off with a thing or two of mine as well, I tell you. My wedding band has gone missing and my dear husband's too, rest his soul. But if you want to know about the wee cats, Miss, you must ask the groundskeeper. He's working in the barn this morning. He knows a thing or two more about them than do I."

The Barnyard

The groundskeeper is a weathered old salt and proudly told me that he had served as ship's mate aboard the Flying Tiger. When he grew too old to sail, Uncle Katt asked him to retire to the manor. Because my uncle was fond of him, he was the only member of the crew privy to the secret cargo in the captain's cabin. "Cap'n called the tiny things his Flittens," he told me, with a smile and a twinkling eye. "And he hunted for them in every corner of the globe. Treated them like precious cargo, he did, until he got them safely back home."

Moored one night near Ceylon, the ship was suddenly boarded by pirates, but the captain and crew fought bravely and overcame them. It was during this heated battle that the tiny mice first came aboard, "and they have made nuisances of themselves ever since," he said.

Flittens gather to watch the milking. Sometimes, the groundskeeper intentionally misses the bucket, and they eagerly lap puddles on the floor or milk splashed onto their fur. He often sets a dish for them in the corner of the barn.

The mice had learned many sneaky and dastardly behaviors aboard the pirate ship, and Uncle and crew could never outsmart or be rid of them. When the Flittens arrived at Mewingham Manor, the tiny mice did too, and have since been their constant, and irritating, companions.

The groundskeeper helped Uncle find the perfect spot at the manor that was most similar to the natural habitats of each of the many types of winged cat (there is more than one species!). Before Uncle left on what was to be his last voyage, he entrusted the care of his dear Flittens to his loyal first mate.

The flying mice make great sport of swinging on the cow bells, which continue to ring long after they release their hold and swing away. The annoyance of the barn animals just adds to the mice's delight!

Flittens seem to feel safe with baby farm animals, with whom they share a wide-eyed innocence.

The Minis raise racing beetles in the potted ornamentals. They feed them a special nectar that creates unnaturally large, speedy "steeds."

Bug Derby

I have begun a study of the winged mice, which I now, suddenly, see everywhere. I call the species Minimus malamus, to describe both their miniscule size and mischievous nature—but, affectionately, I call them Minis. They are very bright-eyed and alert, dart quickly about, nibble at almost anything they come across, stick their noses into things that are simply none of their business, and generally leave a mess in their wake. Yet, despite their silliness

One Mini on a bug will ride, but two Minis on bugs will race! Unsportsman-like behavior to ensure victory has often been observed.

and bad behavior, they are the most enchanting creatures I have ever seen!

Minis also seem quite intelligent, and I have attempted to teach them a few simple tricks. I gave one a piece of fine silk thread from my sewing basket, and he promptly fashioned reins, climbed on top of a beetle, and raced off with great speed and enthusiasm. This set off a chain reaction, and by end of day, a full-blown bug derby was underway!

Rained out. The yellow and black racing stripes made this crossbreed (of potato bug and rhinoceros beetle) a real eye-catcher on the course.

There appear to be a number of racecourses at Mewingham Manor. "Mudders" are run in the vegetable patch after a shower.

Runaway kite

Playtime at the Manor

I took a short stroll through the pasture today.
There, I came upon a most amusing scene—Flittens
of every shape, size, and color at play!

One small flock took turns hiding and seeking
among the hedgerows and at the edge of the woods.
The Minis were not officially allowed to participate,

This wayward bug derby contestant kept
a Flitten amused for hours.

Some Flittens like to skim across rain
puddles on broad, slippery leaves.

Minis have lovely singing voices,
although I had to strain to hear …
"Ring Around the Rosie"?

but they joined in nonetheless. Many a Flitten's clever hiding place was given away by a Mini circling wildly overhead.

Between games, the players would find shady spots in which to take short "cat naps." Each day, at precisely mid-afternoon—when Cook just happens to put her gingerbread out to cool—they would all fly off toward the manor house in search of some refreshment.

Meadow tag!

A perfect cat's cradle. Flittens love to doze for hours in a warm, snug spot. (Flittens have many kitten-like behaviors.)

May 2, 1875

Each night, since I discovered Uncle Ratt's journals, I retire to the library after dinner and keep lanterns burning long into the early hours as I read about his adventures. As I have always suspected, he was a most extraordinary man.

In 1852, he traveled with a Sherpa guide to the highest peaks of the Himalayas. He was searching for a strange creature described to him by an mariner in Valparaiso. Cook said that this adventure was one of Uncle's favorite tales, and each time he told it, the mountains grew higher, the air thinner, and his situation far more precarious. She said that eventually the staff would find urgent projects needing immediate attention whenever the Captain began his story. In his journals he also writes that he found a Flitten sitting in the fresh footprint of Yeti, and he credits his own survival in the frigid conditions on the mountains to the friendly nature of Yeti, with whom, he claims, he once shared an ice cave during a blizzard.

Writing quill, made from the feather of the Little Owl (Athene noctua)

I was just beginning my

descent from the summit of Everest when

I heard a slight scratching and mewing below me.

There he was, trembling beneath the ledge. I was

near faint from the thin air and the high winds, but

quickly devised a most ingenious system for his capture.

The frail tree trunk cracked and strained, and I thought my days were surely done, but I plunged over the ledge and took hold of the creature. This hardy mountain-dwelling species makes its nest in small caves on the near-vertical slopes. The Sherpas say the Flittens steal straw to build their nests and also pilfer shiny objects. I built a bamboo cage to transport this specimen and another that I found deep in a large footstep that my guide, Tenzing, and I agreed belonged to our friend Yeti.

I am at a loss as to a suitable home for this Himalayan Flitten at the manor, so it may have to be of my own devise.

May 3, 1875

I find no further mention in the journal as to where Uncle housed his Himalayan Flittens, so I set out to find the entrance to the cupola, on the third story of the manor. Surely, this would be the perfect home for a creature so accustomed to heights. I found some evidence of nesting there, but no Flittens.

Cook says these Flittens are the only ones "worth their salt." Fond of heights, they perch atop the tallest furniture in the house, and their long fur picks up dust, dust mites, and, on a few unhappy occasions, a Mini or two. Cook uses yarn to entice the Flittens to and fro along hard-to-reach shelves and mantels. When the cleaning is done, she simply lifts them by the scruff and briskly shakes them clean—after which, they themselves do a more meticulous grooming.

I believe the Himalayan Flitten (Flittenus altitudus) nests in the manor's cupola but spends most of its time outdoors.

May 10, 1875

Today, I took a long walk to inspect the height of spring at Mewingham Manor. After a week of warm weather, the Meadow Buttercups (Ranunculous acris) are in exuberant bloom! When I returned mid-afternoon, I wanted a bit of nourishment, and it was still hours until tea. I went into the kitchen to see what Cook had on hand, but stopped suddenly as I heard a low, rumbling drone in the pantry. (Bees, I thought, hovering too close to the window.) I spied a lovely wedge of Swiss cheese on the shelf and began to hunt for a few biscuits to accompany.

The low, rhythmic drone suddenly turned to an angry buzz. I had unwittingly awakened several snoring Minis, comfortably nestled in the holes in the cheese! I let out a small cry of surprise, which soon brought Cook to my side.

"Aye," she said. "You see what it's come to, Miss. I am sorry to say, I used to keep the cheeses well covered, but I cannot any longer. The wee ones make such a fuss. Without proper rest—and snacks close by when they stir—they be more disagreeable than usual." Cook then confided that she must always bake a double batch of sugar cookies, as the Minis routinely make off with half of them. Cookies are

The Minis don't bother at all about the crumbs.

one of their favorite foods. When two Minis try to share one cookie, they bicker bitterly over who has the biggest piece—so Cook always makes sure there are enough, to avoid the unpleasantness.

On baking day, one cannot walk through Mewingham Manor without crunching cookies underfoot. The clever Minis roll the cookies off the counter to break them into pieces that are easy to transport. They prefer to carry their treats away to enjoy them in the comfort of a linen closet or drawer full of socks. They pout whenever Cook bakes square brownies. The corners can be nibbled off, of course, but this would take time and effort, and Minis are not known for their patience or hard work.

The Mess Maker (Flittenus calamitus) prefers the kitchen and dining room to anyplace else at the manor. In just a few minutes, one or two of these Flittens can wreak havoc on a perfectly set table. Nevertheless, Cook has a soft spot for them as they keep her company while she bakes, so she is quick to blame the Minis instead for accidents and spills.

The Kitchen

Life of the party

Flittens and Minis generally appear to coexist peacefully—except around food. From my hours of observation, I deduce that Flittens are herbivores. Minis, on the other hand, eat anything that is either sweet or well prepared, and preferably both.

Flittens are clumsier than the Minis, as their paws lack the dexterity of little mouse "hands." The clever and opportunistic Minis stay close by the Flittens in order to take advantage of their frequent spills.

Although omnivores (they routinely eat Cook's paté) Minis will not kill for food.

Captain Katt's Mew Ling china

2:45 a.m.

Minis dance with more enthusiasm than skill.

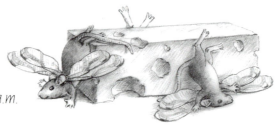

2:46 a.m.

2:47 a.m.

At first, I thought Cook ran a particularly messy kitchen but have since learned she has regular "visitors" that she cannot manage to keep after. Corners are nibbled off the sugar bags, the tea biscuits have ragged edges, unattended teacups are spotted with floury footprints—and those with cream are often found in ruins on the floor. Now I see why she always trims the cheese!

Captain Katt unwittingly brought the Tropical Fruit Tabby home in a shipment of banana trees. These Flittens are "spoilers," nibbling away at many pieces of fruit without ever finishing one.

Sugar lump sculpting

One lump . . . or two?

May 20, 1875

For these past weeks, I have been eagerly anticipating the hatching of the eggs in a wood pigeon nest I found near the barn. There are three eggs, not two—a most unusual occurrence! The groundskeeper told me that he thinks it is time, and urged me to come view the nest right away.

I hurried to the shrub at the edge of the woodlands. I could see, even from some distance, that indeed the eggs had hatched! But at the center of the nest, I saw a tiny, furry creature jostling the nestlings for space. More noteworthy still was the caterwauling of the small creature, as if it expected the mother bird to feed it along with her tender brood. I do not imagine that the diet of the wood pigeon (Columba palumbas) would suit the tiny Flittenus at all.

This newborn is unlike any other I have seen. From the pure white coat, the different-colored eyes, and the high-pitched squawks, I have determined that it must be a rare genetic variation, which even its own relatives cannot recognize. The tiny thing must be seeking the

Evidence of outdoor Flitten infestation. Indoor evidence includes hair in teacups, footprints in frosting, small warm depressions in sock drawers.

company of another flying species—but it is unlikely the mother bird will mistake him for one of her own.

Later, I showed my sketch of the changeling to Cook. Her immediate response was, "Ach! But I know what is on the wee mite's mind. 'Tis squab I'll be having, three nights in a row!" I found her remark most unsettling and think I shall not share my work with Cook again.

She then told me (rather boasting, it seemed to me) that she had just yesterday found a hatchling in a basket of white morels she harvested—perhaps the newborn was a Mushroom Dweller, like the very first Flitten I found. It must be the season for birthing. I will seize the opportunity to document the life cycle of these creatures—perhaps for the first time in the history of science!

The little changeling curled up in this cozy nest for a nap—but the warmth of his body caused the eggs to hatch, and he awoke to quite a racket.

Life Cycle of a Flitten

Flittens follow an insect-like reproductive cycle: egg, caterpillar, pupa, and adult. Eggs have a cat-like shape and dangle from branches on tail-like stalks.

The caterpillar stage

The Flittens eat constantly at this stage, preparing for their pupa hibernation.

I have seen clumps of three to seven pupas under eaves, in the deep shelves of corner cupboards, and in other sheltered areas. The tops of the tubes are sealed shut until the mature Flitten claws its way out. The nascent wings are concealed behind this Flitten's body. A casual observer might mistake abandoned pupa cases for hair balls coughed up by Mr. Grimes.

The wings of all newborn Flittens are various shades of green—to camouflage them among the spring foliage. The wings change color as the Flittens mature. By the time they fly to their respective habitats, the young Flittens will have developed the coloration of their specific species.

Hatchlings congregate for safety and comfort. When they mature, they become very independent and only associate with their own species (although on especially chilly days, I have observed adult Flittens of every type napping in a mound by the hearth).

This Terrrestrial Tabby (Flittenus arboreus) is experiencing the typical post-hatching stage that Cook refers to as "going silly buggers."

Flittens with "robust" physiques take a long time to develop the strength they need to lift their larger-than-average tummies.

May 28, 1875

The orchards are now in full bloom, and the air is scented with the delicate fragrance. The trees are quite old, and their trunks are beautifully gnarled and twisted, covered with lichens and moss. I have identified several ancient varieties of apple (*Malus*), including Catshead and Emperor Alexander (from Russia), and I am already dreaming of Cook's October pies.

Uncle was always hunting for new varieties of fruit trees to bring back to the manor. While in the archipelago of Malay, he discovered an exotic apple tree with juicy bell fruits and wine-red flowers sacred to the goddess of the island. (Captain Bligh himself had brought varieties to Jamaica, and Uncle hoped to cultivate the tender tree here at the manor. He was disappointed to learn he could not—but he did not return home empty-handed.)

A short time later, while searching for drinking water, he came across a new Flitten species, lazing in a pile of leaf litter beneath the Malay apple tree. He prodded and coaxed the sleepy creature into his carrying cage, and headed back to the ship with both *Aqua potabilis* and *Flittenus relaxus* tucked under his arm.

I spent the entire lovely day outdoors, sketching the orchards with a Flitten nestled in the branches of an apple tree nearby.

Cook and the groundskeeper both told me I'd meet Taw River Tom in the orchard. Each fall, Cook and "Wee Tom" compete for the tastiest apples. On especially warm days, the groundskeeper usually finds this Flitten among the fermenting windfall apples, "drunk as a little sailor."

White petals, soft pink blush toward tips of three, also dark pink/fuschia veins

Five inner petals, soft yellow, darker at outside edges, turning very pale then rose/orange at inner throat

Catshead apple tree branch, with three types of lichens

Edge of the Woods

The Terrestrial Tabby (*Flittenus relaxus*) is a singularly lazy species, just as Uncle reported. This model was easy to paint as he held perfectly still for so long. Each of these Flittens lives its entire life in approximately four square meters, beneath the very tree in which it was born.

This slow-moving species prefers a sedentary lifestyle, exhibiting sudden bursts of energy only when feeding. Were it not for their protective coloration (mottled white, brown, and tan), which allows them to blend almost perfectly into their surroundings, the Terrestrial Tabby would be very vulnerable to predation. I often mistake them for tree roots.

All of the Terrestrial Tabby's nutritional needs seem to be met by the oak tree. In the warm months, these Flittens dine heartily on freshly fallen leaves and acorns—no doubt anticipating the winter's less flavorful, dried fare.

The Minis make a contest of staring at the immobile Terrestrial Tabbies, trying to be the first to detect movement.

After seeing the changeling, I now check the contents of every nest I find. I tied my long skirts out of the way (if Mother could have seen me!) and climbed into the tree for a look. All was as it should be.

The Minis delight in teasing the Flittens—and every other small creature in the woodland. After pulling their pranks, they race into tightly curled leaves to hide.

As I watch the dried and twisted leaves stir in the wind, I cannot help but wonder which have indeed been caught by a breeze, and which holds a giggling Mini.

The field mice don't know what to make of their tiny winged relations.

Common kestrel
(Falco tinnunculus)

I tucked a few of these sparrowhawk feathers (Accipiter nisus) into my bonnet. Quite jaunty!

This owl (Tyto alba) nests in the barn at Mewingham Manor.

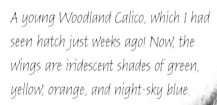

A young Woodland Calico, which I had seen hatch just weeks ago! Now, the wings are iridescent shades of green, yellow, orange, and night-sky blue.

Feather of the male yellowhammer (Emberiza citrinella). The locals sing this bird's song as "a-little-bit-of-bread-and-no-cheese."

The opportunistic Minis find nuts gnawed open by larger rodents and are quite willing to scavenge. Large and very small nibble marks are often visible on the same shell.

Woodland Calico

Uncle discovered this mountain-dwelling species (*Flittenus arboreus*) while traveling through the Andes. When I arrived at the manor in March, I only noticed these creatures inside the house. Suddenly, in early May, I found them in great numbers throughout the grounds. No doubt, they had just returned from the winter migration to their ancestral home in South America.

Like *Flittenus altitudus*, these Flittens love heights. Outdoors, they seek out the highest tree limbs. Indoors, they prefer crown moldings and the tops of armoires. All Woodland Calicos have tri-colored fur. The colors in the wings of the mature adults vary.

Woodland Calicos eat fruits and flowers and seem especially fond of caffeine! Cook says these "little devils" have been known to eat their way through an entire bag of tea in autumn. Perhaps the stimulant keeps them alert during the long winter migration!

A Mini, attempting to hatch this abandoned egg, sat patiently for many hours, wringing his "hands." When the mother bird returned, the Mini looked quite relieved and quickly scampered away.

When toads dream. . . .

June 20, 1875

After his discovery of Flittenus relaxus—his third flitten!—Uncle grew quite curious about the origins of the genus. He believed that the tiny animals were hybrids of some sort, highly evolved, and able to adapt to varied climates and terrain. He suspected that there were many more species living throughout the world, and he made up his mind to find them all.

Uncle read the works of Charles Darwin and many other naturalists, searching for clues, yet found no mention of any creature resembling Flittens. While traveling, he sought the company of the leading thinkers and scientists of the day. Without revealing his great discovery, he tried to learn what he could about the other winged and furry creatures that exist in nature.

Finally, he turned to the ancient texts and found this. In *Historia Naturalis*, written in the first century, B.C., Pliny the Elder described a hedgehog (Echinus) that knocked apples out of trees, so as to impale them on its spines and carry them off. Uncle knew that hedgehogs do not climb trees, so he thought that the great man had made a mistake. How would the bottom-heavy creature ever reach the top limbs of a tree?

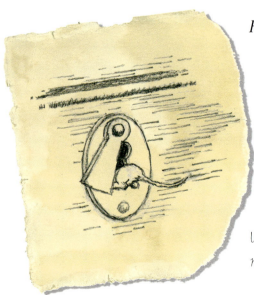

Uncle Katt's drawing of keyhole covers, and a resourceful Mini.

Then, in a volume by Aristotle, Uncle read about a hedgehog that moved "according to the direction of the wind." What concern would the wind be to these burrowing creatures? Uncle asked in the margins of his journal. He soon had his answer—or so he thought. His next journal entry was a scrawled passage that read:

"Today I encountered a small party of Buganda. Noted strange symbols on tribe's bark-cloth attire. Guide translated the symbols from the Bantu as 'winged hedgehog.' From Chwezi legend. The creature wronged the gods, and as punishment, was given wings it could not use. Worn now as symbol of the folly of man. Extinct. Wingless hedgehog skins still revered. Placed on seeds to ensure good harvests."

By the time I finished reading, I had made up my mind to go to London to continue Uncle's research. I know winged cats and mice exist. If, indeed, there once were winged hedgehogs, perhaps there were other winged creatures as well. But what sort? And where? And how? I shall pack at once!

The hedgehog, sacred in China, is also found in Africa, New Zealand, and Great Britain. How to explain such a wide range? Perhaps, at one point, the creature indeed could fly. Yet wouldn't those prickly spines puncture the wings? How could it ever leave the ground? Perhaps there is some truth to the Chwezi legend after all.

Things to Pack:

Magnifying Glass

Notebooks

Reading Glasses

Pastels

Pencils

Ginger Snaps

Umbrella

Native American petroglyph translates to
"Thundercat meets Thundermouse."

The British Museum

Although the staff is busy preparing for the department's move to South Kensington, they have all been most helpful and kind. The earliest evidence I have found here is a fossil dating from the Pleistocene Epoch—although scholars believe it is a composite specimen and not its own genus. Heinrich Schliemann has recently uncovered further evidence of a Flitten-like creature during his excavation of the ancient Greek city of Troy. (Other scientists discount his "evidence" as fake.)

Fossil evidence of the saber-toothed Flitten (Flittenus fatalis), distant relative of the extinct tiger, from the last Ice Age. Obviously, this creature did not have the vegetarian habits of its present-day descendants.

Neferkitty amulet, believed to provide protection against random acts of mayhem.

From the tomb of Neferkitty, one door down from Rameses I in the Valley of the Kings. The name Neferkitty means "the beautiful kitty has come." She was the less popular, younger sister of Nefertiti, the Great Royal Wife of King Akhenaten. As the hieroglyphics here explain, Neferkitty fell out of favor with the royal court because of her belief in tiny winged cats and mice.

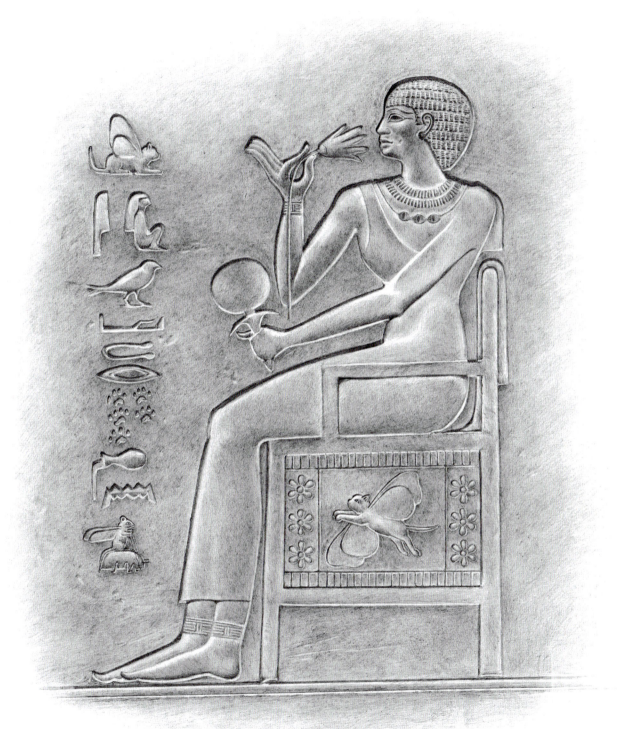

Mandala, fifteenth century. Sanskrit text reveals design was intended for meditation on the blissful state of wingedness. Paw print border signfies the earthly travels of all cats. Four Minis fly in opposite direction of paw prints, indicating a contrary nature. The constellation Leo is evident in the four large petals of a lotus flower (a favorite Flitten food!). According to Indian legends, the winged cats descended from the stars in the night sky.

Bark drawing made by an aboriginal tribe, Torres Strait region, Australia. Very rare. Evidence of a marsupial form of *Flittenus avianus*! Also found many references in native legends and songs. Could these Flittens still exist somewhere?

Cloth from the savannas of northern Cameroon

Motif from Chinese silk embroidery, Tang Dynasty

Motif from an akunitan ("cloth of the great") worn by the chiefs and kings of Africa's Gold Coast

July 18, 1875

How much I missed Mewingham Manor! Cook seemed happy to see me and made a lovely pudding for supper last night. My research went very well, but nothing that I found in London could compare to the discoveries I make every day in my small world here.

I thought about Flitten migration all the way home from London and have developed a theory. I am quite certain that many of the species Uncle collected at the manor continue to migrate each year. Most likely, these travelers return with mates from their native lands and thereby increase the population here at Mewingham.

Before visiting the museum, it had not occurred to me to look for Flittens near the bodies of water around the grounds. I was certain that these furry, flying creatures would share with their earthbound cousins an abhorrence of baths, water, and wet feet. While in London, however, I read many accounts of Flitten lore and sightings in island cultures and water habitats. I decided to have a closer look about the reflecting pool, the trout stream, and the pond.

I was not disappointed. . . .

Bear, frog, and Flitten totem pole found in Kyuquot Sound, Vancouver Island, North America

The Pond

Uncle found the perfect habitat for water-loving Flittens (Flittenus aquaticus). This species loves the food that grows around ponds and streams, especially the water lilies and lotus plants. The aquatic Flittens can execute an admirable dog paddle when necessary, but like their cat cousins, they hate to get their feet wet. Whenever possible, they tiptoe across lily pads, ride on turtles, or catapult on cattails to keep dry.

Alas, at times, the inevitable does occur—but these Flittens have formed close friendships with the other inhabitants of the pond community, and many a time a trout has come to the rescue. I have given these Flittens the common name Trout-Fishing Tabby (although I dare say more often than not it is the trout that does the fishing out!).

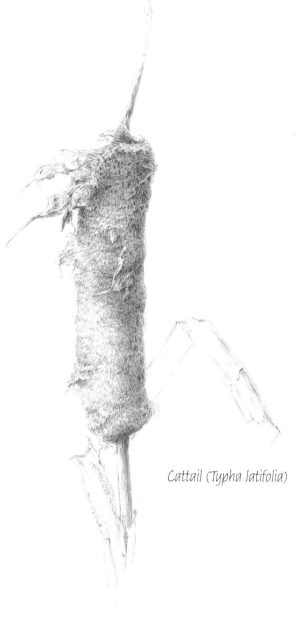

Cattail (Typha latifolia)

These vain Flittens spend hours admiring their reflections in the water and sometimes become so enthralled they topple in! Indoors, I have found them floating on ice chunks in the punch bowl and have become quite adept at scooping them out with a ladle without arousing the suspicion of guests.

Wryly amused frog, watching Flittens struggle to keep dry. Frogs chuckle discretely, but they will never laugh out loud.

Cattails and pussy willows attract this species.

Land snails

A comfortable perch and a captive audience. The water-dwelling Flittens love to hear themselves talk. Fish, turtles, and frogs are perennially cheerful and also very patient. The Flittens' endless chatter simply washes over them, like water rolling off their backs.

August 30, 1875

I wish I could talk with Uncle about his adventures, but I must content myself with his trunk full of journals. I have already read six or seven volumes, and there are still many remaining. Uncle Katt left home for a life at sea at age fourteen, and his younger sister, Kitty—my mother—never knew him well. My grandparents, however, told me all about him.

Even as a boy, Uncle shared my interest in the natural sciences. Grandfather had taught him, as he had taught me, to carefully record every observation, no matter how small and seemingly unimportant, as one might only later discover the true significance of details. Grandfather also showed me Uncle's first childhood sketchbook. It was filled with delightful drawings of butterflies, barn cats, and woodland fairies! Later, as a young man at sea, he faithfully noted his observations in journals. He no doubt referred back to these journals on his voyages.

Tonight I pulled a unique volume from the bottom of the old trunk. It is slightly larger and more worn than most of the other journals, but I recognized at once my uncle's now-familiar hand.

Uncle's painted pill bottles. I found them empty but smelling of some sweet herb. Catnip?

Captain's Log, Merchant Brig Flying Tiger

June 6 Strong breeze. Fine day. Had men put up heavy weather canvas. Crewman Pollard put in irons, drunk on watch, says he's "seen things."

June 7 Wind freshening. Temperature dropping. Hard weather coming. Sign of land. Shortened sail for the night. Pollard still raving in hold.

June 8 Moderate gale. Sailing weather. Single reefed topgallants, the brig is heeling but happy. Mr. Pollard out of irons. Distant Land is uncharted island.

June 10 Fresh gale. Crew is cold. Specimen blown aboard this morning, wings a bit ragged. How he survived the wind is a wonder. I hid him quickly.

June 11 Strong gale. Took in spanker and main course. Fearful to tack in this wind. Full top sails. At 6 bells, Mr. Pollard had a foot rope break and fell from the fore topsail yard. Mr. Atwell asking about yesterday's log entry. I explain a small bird blew aboard, which I later released.

June 13 Fresh breeze. Fine and sunny day but pack ice in distance. More uncharted islands on horizon. I sail to investigate and bring back a full box.

June 14 Strong breeze. Good weather brings good cheer among all. I put Mr. Smith at helm. I've work to do in my cabin.

How I Single-Handedly Procured Felinus Arcticus,

Despite a Series of Unforeseen and Most Unfortunate Mishaps

That Could Not Have Been Otherwise Avoided

I quickly looked through Uncle's journals and found the entries written during the period of the ship's log. It seems that on a harrowing trip to the far north, the Flying Tiger came perilously close to becoming entrapped in the ice. Uncle had ventured from the ship in a small boat to explore an ice floe in Unimak Pass. He was gone so long the ship was delayed in setting sail and was nearly frozen in pack ice for the season. Uncle was searching for an arctic-dwelling Flitten, as he had long ago discovered that—if thorough enough in his search—he would find a new species wherever he looked.

His efforts in the Arctic were rewarded. He found two long-haired Flittens playing in the snow and gently enticed them into his bamboo cage. He also hoisted a large block of ice to take aboard to keep the animals comfortable and cool in his cabin. As he was making his way back to the ship, his trip was hastened by the sudden appearance of a "threatening behemoth standing some 6 meters high."

Flittenus arcticus, or Winter White

When he recounted the tale of his narrow escape to
the men, who had been watching from the shore, none
recalled seeing the creature. One sailor said he had seen
the captain with a young cub, "probably a nursling."

Another saw a few "unsteady penguins" waddling behind as
the captain sped away. "The crew appears skeptical," Uncle
reported, "and asked after my health."

I have not yet seen this arctic species at the manor. Perhaps
these little "snow cats" live in the ice house by the pond. Or maybe they summer in
the north and return to Mewingham Manor when England has a dusting of snow.
I will keep a close watch when the winter months arrive.

Uncle noted that these Flittens become quite giddy at the first signs of snow.
They love to catch snowflakes and slide on the frozen pond. They feast on holly
berries and pine cone seeds. I will have a look in Cook's ice chest, too—although
I would not be pleased to find fur in the ice cream!

Mini snow angels! Cook told me she
usually finds their impressions on the
windowsills, in even the smallest
patches of snow.

September 3, 1875

Relieved by the narrow escape of a winter spent in pack ice, the crew of the Flying Tiger headed south for the equator as quickly as it could sail. Uncle charted course for the islands of the Kingdom of Hawaii. He wanted to search the tropical rainforests for medicinal plants—and more Flittens.

    This is where my uncle found the sweet Flittens that now live in the conservatory. The little creatures nestle in the throats of the most colorful and fragrant blooms. The conservatory is a marvel, well tended by the caretaker, and filled with the most extraordinary specimens of Hibiscus rosa-sinensis and Phalaenopsis, among others. I love to spend early mornings there, and have developed many of my preliminary sketches into full color studies.

Flittenus hibiscus, found by Uncle on the island of Maui

The Conservatory

In his journals, Uncle boasted of the rare orchids he
had found for his conservatory. He said
his collection was "finer than that
of the Queen herself."

After rounding Cape
Horn, he sailed up the
coast of South America to
the mouth of the Amazon. He
moored the Flying Tiger and
traveled upriver in a small vessel
to search for new and exotic
orchid species.

He had filled his boat with
remarkable plants, when he suddenly
spied an enormous bloom more
magnificent than all the others. Risking
life and limb, he climbed out onto a long
sinewy branch to secure it. As he reached for it,

Orchid-dwelling Flittens (Flittenus orchidacaeae) are very
sociable. They sprinkle their stream of mewings with juicy
gossip. The Minis eavesdrop every chance they get.

he discovered a spotted Flitten nestled inside. Despite the increasing peril—snakes, caymans, and piranhas gathered below—he shimmied along the precarious limb. Prepared as always, with the cage hooked over one arm, Uncle retrieved the Flitten, which, along with the orchid (Cattleya eldorado), made the long journey back to Mewingham Manor.

Young Flitten nestled in the roomy bloom of a tiger lily (Lilium tigrinum)

The conservatory is conducive to long, luxurious naps.

Bees are also great gossips. They hang on the Flittens' every word, listening for bits of scandalous news to carry back to the hive.

October 23, 1875

Cook heard again today from Mrs. G——, the seamstress in the village. There have been several more incidents in town recently: small food items gone missing from pantries, plundered stores of biscuits, "misplaced" jewels. Two small children insist that tiny flying kittens are to blame, but Mrs. G—— assured Cook that the tale-tellers were sent to bed early for their fibs. The agitated woman urged Cook to be wary of strangers until the culprits can be found. Yet, Cook and I know well who is behind this mischief.

Flittens can easily camouflage themselves. They are shy and take pains not to be seen, but anyone can see them if they only look closely enough. As I myself have noted on more than one occasion, many fashionable ladies unknowingly transport a Flitten or two in their bonnets.

Our unsuspecting neighbors peer out windows watching for thieves while the Flittens hide in plain view! Even now I hear the faint sounds of fluttering wings——but must look closely to detect the source!

A thimbleful of Mini attempts to startle me.

Uncle loved collecting butterflies. He kept a butterfly net and this portable specimen board—made by the ship's carpenter—in his cabin. He pinned and labeled each specimen as he found it. When he returned to the manor, he transferred them to a glass-front shadow box for permanent display. He must have still been working on these when he left for his final voyage. (The silver automatic pencil is surprisingly well secured.)

Chess set designed by Captain Katt

Appears angelic,
but don't let looks deceive.

The Library

I call the library Flittens "Tiger Swallowtales" because they seem quite gullible and are easily misled by Minis. The Minis have somehow taught themselves to read. I suspect that they tell the Flittens tall tales about what's actually written in books.

The Swallowtales like the smell of paper and ink and spend hours looking at the pictures in books. According to Uncle's journal, these Flittens originated in the ancient libraries of Alexandria. After the libraries were destroyed, the little creatures scattered throughout the civilized world,

The Minis are so naughty that no one will scratch their backs for them.

The Minis never read anything that may improve their minds but will always read my mail.

Tiger Swallowtales live in libraries, bookstores, and on the bookshelves of private homes. They often nestle near illuminated manuscripts. Their wings have the same shape and coloring as the Tiger Swallowtail Butterfly (Papilio glaucus). These Flittens will rustle papers and wiggle long, tassled bookmarks to entice other types of Flittens into the library to play.

128 OF MICE AND MICE

Country Mouse
Country Mice are charming creatures. They rise with the sun and enjoy all of life's simple pleasures. They live in hedgerows, fields, and farmers' cottages. Nature meets their every need. A freshly picked daisy will protect them from the rain. At night, they find shelter under wide mushroom caps. Country Mice love wild nuts and berries and the plain dishes prepared by farmers' wives.

OF MICE AND MICE 129

Church Mouse
Church Mice are the most social of all mice, and the most pious. They read music and speak the tune of every hymn with great emotion. They love church suppers and parishioners that make tasty cheese dishes.

House Mouse
House Mice are known for their cheerfulness. They happily set up housekeeping in any cozy corner. Pantries are favorite spots, as they not only provide warmth from the kitchen but easy access to cookies.

looking for new homes and illustrated books. Uncle acquired them while building his rare book collection. He was in London gathering provisions for his next voyage and made his regular visit to the bookshop on Charing Cross Road. The Swallowtales traveled back to Mewingham Manor in a box of leather-bound volumes of maritime adventures.

At dusk, nocturnal Flittens come awake, emerging from the cool, dark places where they sleep during the day.

Night Life

I have just read Uncle's account of the nocturnal habits of some Flittens. He first observed strange behavior patterns while transporting some from Norway, Land of the Midnight Sun. As the ship traveled beneath the constellation Leo, the Flittens—although well hidden below deck— began to mew in a unified chorus, quietly at first, but then less so. Uncle was forced to sing at the top of his own lungs to drown out the cacophony, so as not to arouse the suspicions of the crew.

I have often wondered about the tiny shadows flickering along my bedroom walls at night and the distant humming that almost sounds like a song.

Tonight, I will keep a closer watch....

The Russian Blue (Flittenus athletus) is adept at outflying the owls and outfoxing the foxes, so they have no fear of the dark. They frequently host all-night parties.

These nocturnal, moth-like Flittens are attracted
to the lights of the manor house at night.
They also love a full moon, the
Northern Lights, and fireflies.

On bright moonlit nights, the Minis gather and twitter in a
most conspiratorial manner. I suspect they are discussing the
contents of my most recent correspondence—and most
certainly spreading unflattering rumors.

The resourceful Minis, who hate to miss a
thing, have no trouble navigating at night.

Minis nest in chinks in the mortar of the ruin's entrance gate. The stones are covered with lichens and moss that have accumulated over centuries.

The Mysterious Ruins

At the furthest edge of the estate, concealed behind a thick row of hemlock, there is a clearing I want to explore. I have avoided this place because it appears so forbidding and forsaken. As I was observing the nighttime activities of the Flittens, I saw shadows circling over the crumbled foundation of what must have been the original manor house. I asked the groundskeeper about the ruins. Mysteriously, he called it "the gathering place."

He told me that the spot is well known among Flittens, as a sort of way station for the migrating species. Word has spread far and wide of Mewingham Manor's hospitable residents. Many of the travelers have such a good time that they delay resuming their trip. Others reconsider their travel plans entirely and decide simply to remain.

To me, the ruins sound to be quite an inviting place. Perhaps there is nothing to dread at all. I resolved to muster my courage, wait until dark, and have a look around.

A Russian Blue, flying with young bats? Migrating Flittens usually fly so high that they are not visible from the ground.

Wistful Natterjack toad (Bufo calamita)

The Log Dweller (Flittenus sylvanus) prefers old-growth trees. Ancient hollowed logs and stumps are perfect for long, cool naps. This Mini is trying to engage the sleepy Flitten in some silly game—but is having no luck. I think I have also seen this species indoors, sleeping in the wood bin near the hearth.

As I sketched this owl feather caught on a thistle, a hawk circling overhead cast a shadow on the ground.

Call of the wild! The Minis have an eerie howl. They promote the notion that the ruins are best avoided after dark . . . but why?

Christmas, 1875

The Minis convinced some of the younger Flittens that THEY would make lovely ornaments. I had to "unhook" several whose wings got stuck on the boughs. Once the flurry of decorating activity was over, we all stepped back to admire the sparkling tree.

What a joyous place to be in such a joyous season! Cook has been merrier than I have ever seen her, bustling to and fro, covered with jams and flour, readying the great feast! The others have been diligently rehearsing carols—the Flittens are completely tone-deaf, but that does not keep them from caterwauling along. I have festooned the mantels with garlands of fresh juniper and hung the mistletoe (a few amorous Minis moved in right away, and they have not left since).

Of course, I have invited the staff and their families to join in the festivities at the manor. I also invited Sir Percy, Uncle's solicitor, who has been so kind to me these many months. (I wonder what he knows of Uncle's secret collection?) I am sure Uncle would have been pleased to see the house filled with laughter, music, and high spirits! I just hope my tiny companions will be on their best behavior— and stay out of the punch bowl!

Even with their fine, strong voices, Cook and the groundskeeper could barely be heard over the din of the Minis' squeaking.

Cook's glazed cookies were difficult to explain to the guests—but the staff and I had a good chuckle. Fortunately, the shape deterred the Minis from rolling them off the serving trays.

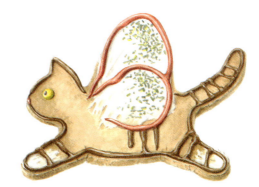

Cook and I strung popcorn and cranberries for the tree, which was slow going, as the Minis ate more than their share. We had to stop often to replenish our supply.

Getting some help with the gift wrapping

Finally, Cook suggested the Minis could pop their own corn. Afterward, the silver teaspoons, black from candle smoke, had to be thoroughly polished.

January 18, 1876

A parcel arrived in today's post from Sir Percy. In the letter enclosed, he again expressed his gratitude for the fine party on Christmas Day. "It was a pleasure," he wrote, "to see the manor full of so much life." I stopped for a moment to wonder at this last bit, then read on.

Now that I had been living at Mewingham Manor for some time, he explained, and had settled in so nicely, as he had hoped I would, he was sending a letter my uncle had meant for me to have. Uncle had charged him with delivering it only if I remained at Mewingham Manor and was as devoted to it as he had been, "as I am now most confident that you are," Sir Percy wrote. He admitted that he himself did not know the contents of the letter, as Uncle had wished to maintain the strictest confidence.

I turned the envelope over in my hands several times, savoring the anticipation of reading my uncle's words, this time intended for me. I noted the insignia imprinted in the wax—the tiny paw prints across a coat of arms. My heart nearly stopped beating as I broke open the seal.

The daguerrotype enclosed. The notation reads, "A short nap in the orchard with friends, Mewingham Manor, 1871."

MEWINGHAM MANOR

August 4, 1871

My dear Edwina,

Forgive me for not welcoming you myself to Mewingham Manor, which would have been my delight, but by now you understand that circumstances have made that quite impossible.

As I set forth on what will be my greatest adventure, I have instructed Sir Percy that, in the event of my untimely death or disappearance, you are to become the sole mistress of Mewingham Manor and all its contents and inhabitants, the place and creatures I have most loved on Earth.

Through the years, Sir Percy—a most faithful correspondent—has kept me well informed of your aspirations in the field of natural sciences. He has sent me your ambitious articles and drawings from the London journals. Truly, we are kindred spirits, and you are the one person to whom I can bequeath my treasure.

Many, including Percy, have cautioned me against returning to the Amazon—a long and grueling expedition for a man of my advanced years, and there are other dangers as well—but I assure you I have sound reasons. Many years ago I had a glimpse of the most remarkable species, which since has eluded me again and again. I will not rest until I find it and learn its great secrets. It is a creature unlike any other, of a nature that not even genius can describe.

This letter is in your hand because I have failed. I ask that you take up my quest for me, dear niece, and fulfill my life's ambition. You will never regret it. This rare and exceptional creature will change your life, as I had hoped it would mine, and ours together, had we the good fortune to meet in this earthly sphere.

You may turn with confidence to Sir Percy should you have any practical needs. Farewell, dear Edwina, and safe return.

Truly yours,

Captain Bartholomew Katt

Off to the Amazon . . .

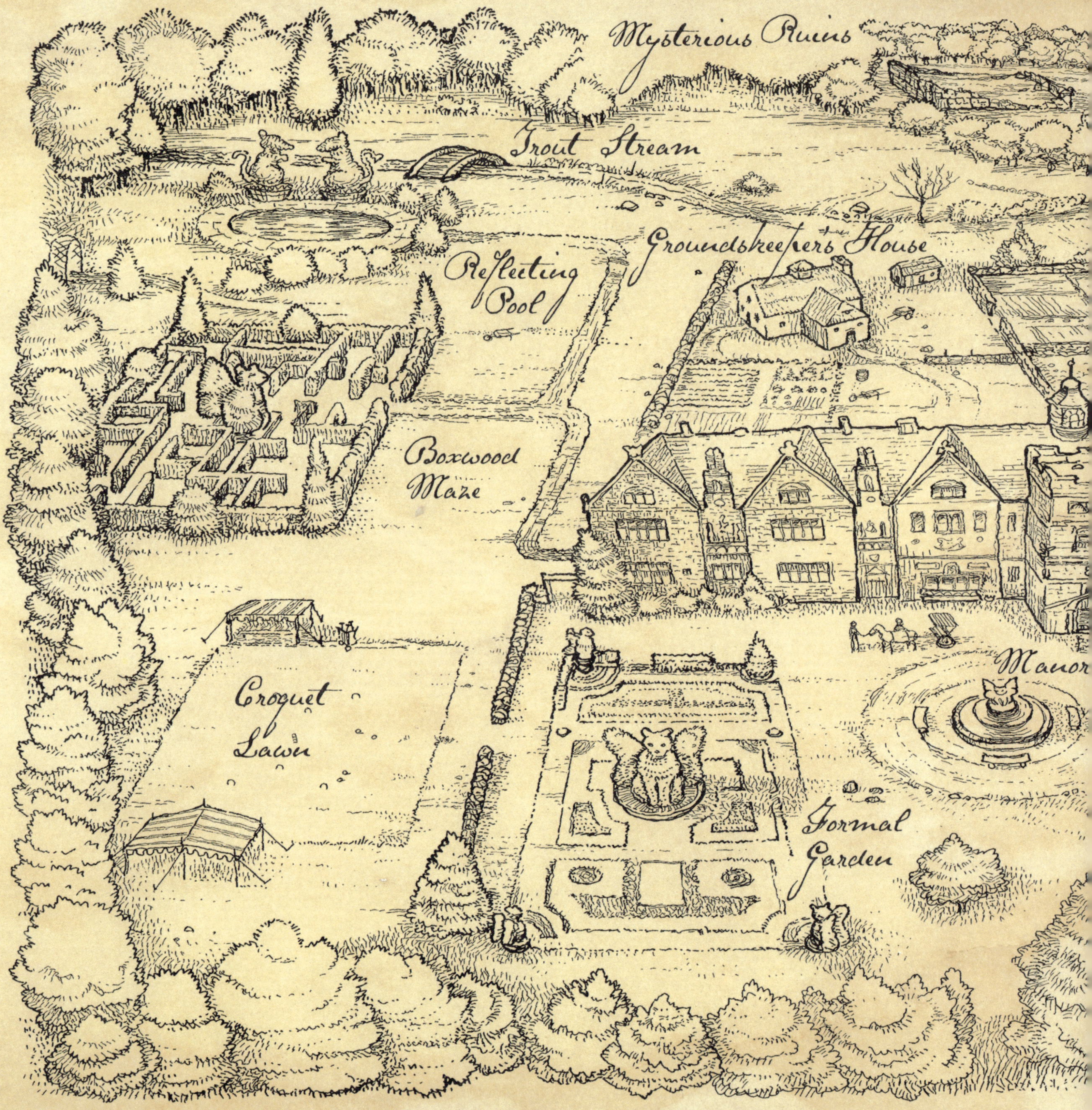

Mysterious Ruins

Trout Stream

Reflecting
Pool

Groundskeeper's House

Boxwood
Maze

Manor

Croquet
Lawn

Formal
Garden